Hans Christian Andersen

The Brave Tin Soldier

and other fairy tales

Miles
Kelly

First published in 2015 by Miles Kelly Publishing Ltd
Harding's Barn, Bardfield End Green, Thaxted, Essex, CM6 3PX, UK

2 4 6 8 10 9 7 5 3

Publishing Director Belinda Gallagher
Creative Director Jo Cowan
Editorial Director Rosie Neave
Editor Amy Johnson
Designers Rob Hale, Joe Jones
Production Elizabeth Collins, Caroline Kelly
Reprographics Stephan Davis, Jennifer Cozens, Thom Allaway
Assets Lorraine King

ISBN 978-1-78209-752-5

Printed in China

British Library Cataloguing-in-Publication Data
A catalogue record for this book is available from the British Library

ACKNOWLEDGEMENTS
The publishers would like to thank the following artists who have contributed to this book:

Front cover and all border illustrations: Louise Ellis (The Bright Agency)

Inside illustrations:
The Brave Tin Soldier Martina Peluso (Advocate-art)
The Fir Tree Christine Battuz (Advocate-art)
It's Quite True! Mónica Carretero (Plum Pudding Illustration Agency)
The Nightingale Claudia Venturini (Plum Pudding Illustration Agency)

Made with paper from a sustainable forest

www.mileskelly.net
info@mileskelly.net

Contents

The
Brave
Tin Soldier

One Christmas, a little boy was given a dull-looking box as a present. But when he opened it, he was delighted. Inside were twenty-five tin soldiers. They wore smart red-and-blue uniforms and looked straight ahead, shouldering their guns. They were brothers, because they had all been made out of the same old tin spoon. And they were all exactly alike except for one – he had only one leg, for he had been the last one to be made and there hadn't been enough tin to finish him off.

The little boy started playing with his new toys straight away. He arranged them on a table where there was a little cardboard castle. In front of the castle were model trees surrounding a piece of mirror for a lake, which had paper swans swimming on it.

At the open door of the castle stood a tiny lady. She was also a cardboard cut-out, but she wore a proper dress of floaty material, with a blue ribbon shawl around her shoulders, fixed in place with a glittering tinsel rose. The little lady was a dancer and she stretched out her arms and raised one leg so high that, from where the one-legged tin soldier was standing, he couldn't see it at all. He thought that she, like himself, had only one leg.

'That is the wife for me,' he thought. 'But she is grand and lives in a castle, while I have only a box to live in with my twenty-four brothers – that's no good for her.' Still, the one-legged tin soldier was determined to get to know her somehow.

When the little boy came down to play next morning, he lined up the tin soldiers

along the windowsill. But alas, the window was open. A gust of wind set a curtain fluttering, which caught the one-legged tin soldier and knocked him out. Down, down, down he fell, head over heel, and landed in the street below.

He lay there and was rained on. When the shower was over, two boys passed by and spotted him. They made a boat out of paper and placed the tin soldier in it, and sent him sailing down the gutter while they ran alongside, shouting with excitement. The paper boat rocked up and down, and sometimes span round so quickly that the tin soldier trembled. Yet he did not let his fear show – his face didn't flicker, he just looked straight before him with his gun shouldered, standing to attention.

Suddenly the boat shot into a drain and then it was as dark as the tin soldier's box. 'Where am I going now?' he thought. 'If only the little lady were here with me, I would not mind the darkness.'

Out of the shadows a great water-rat loomed. "Have you got a passport?" he demanded. "Show it to me at once." But the tin soldier remained silent and to attention, holding his gun tighter than ever.

The boat sailed on in the gloom of the tunnel, the strong current carrying it forward. The rat followed it, gnashing his teeth and shouting out, "Stop, you have not shown your passport!"

All at once the soldier saw
the end of the drain approaching fast. Up
ahead, the stream became a waterfall, which
tumbled steeply down into a canal, back into
daylight. The poor tin soldier held himself as
stiffly as possible to show that he was not
afraid. His boat shot over the falls, filled with
water and began sinking in the canal. As the

water closed over his head, he thought of the beautiful little dancer whom he would never see again.

The soldier was quickly swallowed up by a fish. How dark it was! But still he stood firm. The fish swam to and fro for what seemed like days – then the tin soldier felt him become quite still. He waited… and waited… and finally daylight opened over him. A voice cried out, "I don't believe it, here is the missing tin soldier!"

The fish had been caught, taken to the market and sold to the little boy's mother, who took him home and cut him open to cook him for tea. She cleaned the soldier and carried him into the little boy's room. She put him back on the table and there he was with his brothers again, back where he could gaze at the beautiful little dancer.

Unfortunately, the tin soldier didn't look the same after his adventures. The bright colours had been washed from his uniform. Later that day, the little boy picked him up and threw him onto the open fire in the hearth. The tin soldier lay there, still smartly to attention as the flames licked around him, his eyes fixed firmly on his beloved dancer.

Next morning, lying in the ashes of the fire, the boy's mother found a little tin heart.

The Fir Tree

Out in the forest stood a pretty little fir tree. He grew in a lovely sunny spot, but he was not happy. He longed to grow tall, like all the other firs round about. Sometimes little children would come by, gathering strawberries and raspberries. They would say, "Oh how sweet that little tree is!" – but it just made the tree really fed up.

"Oh, if only I were as tall as the other trees," sighed the little fir, "I would spread my branches far around and look out over the whole wide world. The birds would nest in me and when the wind blew I could nod grandly like the others."

Months passed and the little fir took no pleasure in the sunshine, the birds and the clouds that went sailing over him morning and evening. Then winter came, and the snow lay all around, white and sparkling. A hare often came bounding along and would spring right over him. It made him so angry!

But by the time two more winters had passed, the little fir had grown. The hare could no longer leap over him.

'To grow up and become old and important – that's the best thing in the world,' thought the tree.

Every autumn, woodcutters came and felled a few of the largest trees. Each year, as the little fir grew taller, he shuddered with fear when it happened. For the great, stately trees fell to the ground with a crash and their branches were cut off. Then they were laid on carts and horses dragged them away out of the wood. 'Where are they going?' the fir tree always wondered.

"Enjoy being young!" the sunbeams told him, and the wind gave him kisses – but the tree just shrugged them off.

When Christmas time came around, still more trees were felled – sometimes quite young ones, even smaller than the fir tree, now he had grown. The woodcutters never hacked off their branches – but still, they were loaded onto carts and horses dragged them away. "What happens to them?" the fir tree thought aloud.

"We know!" chirped the swallows. "People take them into their houses and decorate them with colourful ornaments and brightly shining candles. They are so beautiful!"

"If only I could be one of them one day," sighed the fir.

"Be content here in the fresh woodland," said the raindrops.

"It is better out here with us," squeaked the squirrels.

But the fir could not be content. He longed to be elsewhere – and he grew and grew and grew.

The next Christmas time, the fir tree was felled before any of the others. He was taken away into a yard where there were hundreds of other felled trees. Then a man came and picked him out and carried him off to his house. Inside, he was placed in a big tub, in a warm room, and all around him were chairs, vases and pictures.

How the tree trembled with excitement! What was to happen now?

Children soon came and decorated him, until he sparkled and glittered and gleamed. He stood tall and proud at first, but after a few days, his branches grew so tired with holding up all the decorations that he developed quite a backache! 'When will this be over?' he wondered.

Then one afternoon people flocked into the

room for a party. There were games, and singing and dancing, and storytelling – and they all gave each other presents from around the tree's big tub. But how noisy it was for the tree, who was used to the gentle sighing of the wind, the songs of the birds and the snuffling of the woodland creatures.

At last everyone went home and the candles were blown out, leaving the tree alone all night, quiet and thinking of the forest.

Next morning, a lady came and stripped the fir tree's branches bare of all the decorations. She wrapped them up in newspaper and packed them away into boxes. Then the man who had brought the tree to the house heaved him up out of the tub. He dragged him outside into the courtyard and flung him into a corner among some nettles and weeds.

"At last, I am outside again!" said the tree to himself. He stretched out his branches towards the pale winter sunshine, but alas! They had become brown and dry. His needles dropped off and fell like rain to the ground. "Oh, I wish had made the most of life when I was younger," he sighed. "Everyone told me to be happy, but I just wanted to grow up. Now I am old – and I haven't

stopped to enjoy anything at all."

Next day, a boy came and chopped the tree into little pieces for the fire.

The tree's life was past – and the story is past too, for that's the way with all stories.

21

It's Quite True!

Once upon a time, there was a farmyard in which chickens bustled about, pecking and scratching. When the sun set, the chickens scuttled into the hen house and jumped up on their perches to roost.

One of them was a hen with unusual speckled feathers. One evening, as she flew up to roost, she pecked herself with her beak and a little feather fell out. She didn't mind at all. In fact, seeing it made her think of a little joke that she had heard.

"Which side of a chicken has more feathers?" she asked herself. "The outside!" And she chuckled quietly. "Ah, never mind – the more feathers I lose, the more lovely I become," she murmured merrily, and settled down to sleep.

But the chicken that sat next to the speckled hen did not doze off. Instead, she remained awake, thinking about what she had just heard.

"Well I never," she said, pecking her neighbour on the other side awake. "Do you know what I've just heard? There's a hen here who wants to peck her feathers out to look beautiful! I don't think that will work, do you? The cockerel won't like her like that, will he? In fact, I would have thought it would put him right off her!"

The sleepy chicken she was talking to didn't take much notice, she just tucked her head under her wing and went back to sleep. But swooping around the outside of the hen house was a mother owl, with her husband and her little owlets. The family had very sharp ears and they heard everything that the neighbour chicken had said.

"Did you hear that?" the mother owl remarked to the father owl. "There is a hen in there who has gone totally mad. She pulls out all her feathers and then parades about in front of the cockerel, thinking he's going to admire her."

"Toowhit-toowhoo!" cried the father owl in alarm. And he flew off to tell the doves in the dovecote in the neighbouring farmyard down the lane.

"Toowhit-toowhoo!" the father owl screeched to the doves. "Have you heard the news? There's a hen who has pulled out all her feathers, thinking that the cockerel will think she's beautiful. She's going to die of cold – in fact, she may be dead already!"

"Oh goodness, that's dreadful," cooed the doves. "Where? Where?"

"In the farmyard down the road. I've just been there myself. I know it's not right to spread gossip, but it's all true, I tell you!"

"Oooh we believe you, we do," cooed the

doves, and they flew into their own farmyard. "Listen, everyone!" one of the doves called. "Down the road, at the next farm, there's a hen who has plucked out all her feathers—"

"In fact, I think the owl told us there were two!" another dove interrupted.

"Anyway," the first dove went on, "both of them caught a terrible cold – and now they're dead!"

The cockerel heard every word of what the doves had said and his eyes opened wide. 'Well, I guess it's up to me to spread the news,' he thought to himself. So he flapped up on top of the hen house and crowed, "Cockadoodledoo! Three hens from the farm down the road have plucked out all their feathers, trying to look beautiful for the cockerel, and they have died!"

All the animals in the farmyard heard it, even the rats, who scuttled further down the road to the next farmyard.

"Have you heard?" they squeaked. "Five hens had a competition to win the love of a cockerel. They plucked out all their feathers, to see who looked best without them. But they argued and started a fight, then they pecked each other to death!"

And so the animals and birds passed on the story from farmyard to farmyard, and each time it was told it became more fantastical than the last. In the end, the tale came back to the farmyard in which it began.

"Did you know," cried a ladybird who brought the news, "a whole flock of hens went mad and pecked out each other's feathers, then killed the cockerel?"

"Oh heaven save us!" gasped the speckled

hen – who of course did not recognize her own story at all.

"It's quite true!" insisted the ladybird.

And that's where the saying comes from: One little feather can swell until it becomes a whole flock of chickens.

The Nightingale

The emperor of China lived in the most splendid palace in the world. It was surrounded by a large, beautiful garden that ended in a mighty forest which stretched down to the sea. There lived a nightingale.

Its song was so beautiful that the fishermen would stop to listen on their way out to fish on the ocean.

Travellers came from all over the world to see the emperor's city and his palace and garden, but when they heard the nightingale, they would say: "That is most beautiful thing of all." They even wrote it down in books about their adventures.

One of these books reached the hands of the emperor one day. He sat in his golden chair reading the glowing descriptions of his city, nodding his head. Then he read the words: "The nightingale is best of all."

"What is this?" he said. "A nightingale! I have never heard of such a bird. Yet this book says it's the most wonderful thing in my empire – and it lives in my garden, too!"

He summoned the royal chamberlain to find the bird.

"Fetch this nightingale," the emperor demanded. "I command it to sing for me this evening."

The royal chamberlain raced through the palace, accompanied by half the court, all searching for the nightingale.

At length they came to the kitchen, where a little maid exclaimed, "I know the nightingale!" And she led everyone out into the wood.

"There it is!" said the girl, and she pointed to a dingy little bird up in the boughs.

"That's it?" exclaimed the royal chamberlain. "It looks so dull – maybe it's so frightened at the sight of us that it's lost all its colour."

"Dear nightingale," called the little girl, "the emperor would like you to sing to him."

"My song sounds best here in the wood," said the nightingale, "but of course I will come," and he accompanied everyone back through the trees.

At the palace, the nightingale sang so

gloriously that the emperor wept. He commanded that the nightingale would stay at court, and he put him in a cage. The nightingale was allowed out twice a day and once at night, when a servant held a string attached to his leg so he couldn't fly away.

The poor nightingale was very sad…

One day a box arrived for the emperor, with the words, 'A gift from the Emperor of Japan,' written on the outside.

Inside was an incredible clockwork nightingale, decorated all over with jewels. When it was wound up it sang and its glittering tail moved up and down.

"How perfect!" the royal chamberlain cried in delight, admiring it from all angles.

"Now we must hear the two birds sing together!" the emperor said. But it did not sound as lovely as he thought, for the real bird sang whatever came into its little throat, while the artificial bird knew just one melody.

So then the new one was wound up to sing by itself. Everyone clapped it just as much as they clapped the real bird. Besides, it was much more beautiful.

Over again, for thirty-three times, it sang the same tune. Then the emperor said: "Let's hear the real bird on its own now."

But where was the nightingale? No one had noticed it fly out of the open window.

"How ungrateful, after I gave him a splendid cage to live in!" exclaimed the emperor, extremely cross. "I never want to see the real bird again!" From then on, he kept the clockwork nightingale on a satin cushion close to his bed and he ordered him to be wound up to sing several times a day.

One evening the emperor lay in his bed listening to the bird singing. Suddenly, it stopped with a jerk. *Bang!* Something snapped inside, its wheels ran down with a whirr, and then there was silence.

The emperor sent for a watchmaker at once. After he had examined its clockwork a great deal, he managed to get it going again.

"You must not use it too much," the watchmaker warned, "it is nearly worn out, so the music won't be as good."

Then the emperor announced that the bird would be wound up to sing just once a year.

Years went by and the emperor fell very ill. The time came when he lay in his bed with the clockwork bird on the cushion next to him, and he was so still that all the courtiers thought he was dead. Sadly, they hung their heads and went away.

But the emperor was still alive – only just. He opened his eyes and gasped: "I want to hear music one last time!"

But no one was there to help him. The clockwork bird was silent, for unless someone wound it up, it could not sing.

Suddenly a silvery note floated in at the window. It was the voice of the real nightingale, on a branch outside. It had heard that the emperor was very ill and had come back to comfort him.

As the emperor listened to the little bird's song, he felt warmth and energy flowing through him. He started to feel better and as if he would recover.

"Little bird, how can I

thank you?" he wept. "Please say you will stay with me again. You can fly away to wherever you want, whenever you want, and I will break the clockwork bird into pieces."

"Don't do that," said the nightingale, "it has done its best – keep it. I cannot live inside the palace for it makes me unhappy, but I will come to you every evening and sing outside your window." And so saying, he flew away.

When the servants entered to take the dead emperor away, they instead found him standing there, strong and well.

"Morning!" the emperor said, cheerfully.